First published in *Fairy Tales* 2000 by Walker Books Ltd
87 Vauxhall Walk, London SE11 5HJ

This edition published 2003

2 4 6 8 10 9 7 5 3 1

This book has been typeset in Palatino

Printed in China

British Library Cataloguing in Publication Data:
a catalogue record for this book is available from the British Library

ISBN 0-7445-9875-3

www.walkerbooks.co.uk

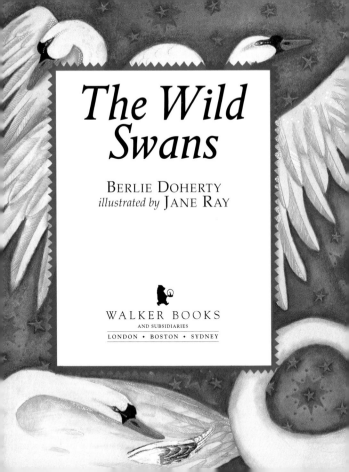

The Wild Swans

BERLIE DOHERTY

illustrated by JANE RAY

WALKER BOOKS

AND SUBSIDIARIES

LONDON · BOSTON · SYDNEY

A long time ago there were a king and queen who had eleven sons. One winter's day when the queen was in her garden she saw a bird with black wings, and a bush with berries as red as blood against the white snow, and she said out loud, "How I wish I had a daughter whose skin was as white as that snow, and whose lips were as red as those berries, and whose hair was as black as that bird's wings. How I would love her!"

And instantly an old woman with long grey hair like feathers appeared at

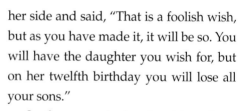

her side and said, "That is a foolish wish, but as you have made it, it will be so. You will have the daughter you wish for, but on her twelfth birthday you will lose all your sons."

So the queen had a daughter whose skin was as white as snow, and whose hair was as black as a raven's wing, and whose lips and cheeks were as red as berries. "I name you Snow-rose," the queen said. All her brothers loved her and throughout her childhood they played together in the gardens of the castle. But on the night of Snow-rose's twelfth birthday the queen remembered what the old woman had said.

"We must make our sons safe," she told her husband. "We must lock them inside a tower where no harm can come to them."

But there was a window open in the tower, and just as the day was ending there was a sudden rushing and beating of wings and with a strange, sad cry eleven swans flew out into the night and streamed out over the great trees of the castle grounds.

Far below them they could see the castle where their sister was sleeping, and they drifted down towards it, craning their long necks and flapping their great wings.

"Snow-rose!" they called. "Goodbye, Snow-rose."

Snow-rose dreamed about her brothers but didn't know they were there, changed into swans and gliding above her rooftop. When day came they soared up again, high into the air. They flew through many nights and many days until they came to a dark forest stretching down to the sea, and there they landed.

When Snow-rose discovered that her brothers had gone, and that she was the cause to it, she begged to be allowed to follow them.

"Ah, no," said the queen. "Don't go. I dread in my heart that I might lose you, too."

But Snow-rose grieved for a year and a day for her lost brothers. And one night when the moon was like a silver boat she let herself out of the castle and ran away to find them.

She wandered for days through the fields and woods, along the whispering rivers, and when she came to the forest it was so dark and deep that she thought she would never see the light of day again. She was hungry and cold and very tired, but when she slept she dreamed that she was with her brothers and that they were playing together in the castle. When she woke up and saw how dark and huge the forest was, she was more afraid than ever, until glow-worms came to light up the grasses around her, and that brought her some comfort.

In the dim grey morning Snow-rose heard someone coming towards her through the trees. She hid and saw an old woman with hair like feathers, carrying a basket of berries, and begged her to give her some.

"I'm looking for my brothers," she told the woman. "Have you seen eleven princes riding through here?"

"No," the old woman said. "But go down as far as the shore and you will see something that will remind you of your brothers."

So Snow-rose thanked her and went down to the edge of the forest, and there was a wide ocean stretching away from her as far as she could see. She walked along the shore and found eleven swan feathers. She gathered them up, wondering, and as soon as she held them all in her hands she heard a beating of wings and eleven swans circled in the sky above her head, and when darkness was just beginning to fall the swans came down on to the shore and changed into eleven young men, and she recognized them as her brothers.

The girl was filled with joy that she had found them again, but they told her that all through the hours of daylight they had to fly without resting, and by night they changed into young men again, and as soon as day broke they became swans, flying, flying without rest. Her heart was full of pity for them, and she cried because so much suffering had come to them on her account.

"Don't be sad for us," said the youngest brother, her favourite. "We came back hoping to see you, and we have done.

But we can't stay any longer than one night on your land. We have our own land now, far away across this sea. We have to go back there at dawn."

"Then take me with you," Snow-rose begged.

So all night without resting they gathered rushes and wove a basket for her, and as soon as day broke and they became swans again the brothers lifted her up into the sky, and the youngest brother flew above her to shield her eyes from the sun.

They flew through all the hours of day, but by dusk they were tiring. Very soon they would turn into young men again. If they didn't find somewhere to land they would fall out of the sky and

drown. At last the youngest brother spied a rock sticking like a seal's head out of the sea, and they landed just in time. The tips of their wing feathers floated away on the dark water. They clung to each other on the tiny rock, too afraid to sleep, and when day came they rose up again, and soared right into the heart of the deepest clouds, where rainbows shone and their reflections glimmered like dazzling ghosts.

They came to land on a beautiful shore near a towering castle. Here they made their home. Even so, Snow-rose only saw her brothers at night. By day they circled the sky or floated over the waves. Snow-rose stood on the shore, gazing after them.

"If only I could help them!" she said out loud, and instantly the old woman appeared at her side.

"If you really mean that, there is a way," the old woman said. "And you are the only person who can do it."

"What is it? I don't mind how hard it is."

"It is very hard," the old woman assured her. She showed Snow-rose a bunch of stinging nettles that she had in her hand. "These nettles grow all around here. You must gather them with your bare hands, and tread them into flax with your bare feet, and then weave them into eleven coats of mail, each for one of your brothers. Can you bear to do that?"

"Yes, I can," Snow-rose said at once.

"And during all this time you must never say a word," said the old woman, turning away. "Or cry, or sing, or laugh. If you do any of these things, your brothers will be wild swans until the day they die." And with that, she was gone.

Straight away Snow-rose ran round the fields gathering nettles with her bare hands. When her brothers returned that night they were distressed to see her sitting by candlelight with great red weals and blisters across her hands and her feet, and with not a word to say to any of them.

"Snow-rose, what's happened to you?" they asked her. "Please tell us." But she wouldn't say a word.

Every day was the same. They couldn't understand her silence. Their only consolation was that she seemed to be quite happy in her task of gathering nettles and weaving the flax she made from them, and when she finished her first coat of mail her eyes shone with joy.

One morning some hunters were riding by. They saw the beautiful girl alone and busy at her task, and called their prince over to see her. He fell in love with her, and came every day to see her, just sitting by to watch her sewing.

"Come with me to the castle," he asked her. "Will you marry me?"

She said nothing at all to him, and he took her silence for consent and lifted her up on his horse. She could say nothing,

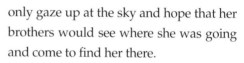

only gaze up at the sky and hope that her brothers would see where she was going and come to find her there.

When they arrived at the castle the prince showed her to her room, and Snow-rose was overjoyed to see that her nettles and her weaving had been brought for her by one of the huntsmen. "This is to remind you of the kind of life you used to lead," the prince told her, and was amused to see her sitting down straight to her task, as if nothing else mattered to her.

Everybody who saw Snow-rose loved her because of her beauty. Everyone, that is, except for the prince's mother. She was sure that the girl was a woodman's daughter, and she was furious that her son had brought a common speechless girl into her castle. "You're not good enough for him!" she hissed. "I'll show him how worthless you are!"

So when Snow-rose was bathing in the stream, the queen took three toads and told them to sit on the girl's head and neck and shoulders.

"Make her as ugly as you are!" she said to one, and to another, "Make her as sluggish as you are!" and to the third, "Make her as bad-tempered as you are and then the prince will hate her!" But the girl was too good and innocent for the magic spell to work on her, and as soon as the toads touched her they turned into red flowers and floated away.

And still Snow-rose wove her coats of mail, all day and all night, by moonlight and candlelight. Nothing would keep her from her task. Soon she had run out of nettles, and she took to leaving the castle at night in search of more. The very best nettles were in the graveyard. She knew that was where the witches liked to meet, around the newly dug graves, where it was said they would eat anyone, alive or dead.

Snow-rose was very frightened, yet she desperately needed the nettles, so she crept out there in the still of the night. But the queen saw the light of her candle through the window one night and decided to follow her, and when she saw her kneeling down in the graveyard surrounded by cackling witches she ran to the prince and woke him up.

"That girl you have brought home is a witch!" she said in triumph. "Come and see!" And the prince came and saw for himself the newly turned earth, and the ring of witches, and Snow-rose kneeling among them, and he had to believe what he saw. "If you are innocent, say so!" he begged her. Snow-rose said nothing.

"Then she must be guilty," the prince said, with sorrow in his heart.

"Throw her in jail!" the queen ordered.

Now in that country witches, if they were caught, were burnt to death, and that was the punishment that the wicked queen demanded for the girl. Snow-rose

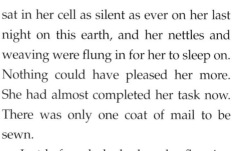

sat in her cell as silent as ever on her last night on this earth, and her nettles and weaving were flung in for her to sleep on. Nothing could have pleased her more. She had almost completed her task now. There was only one coat of mail to be sewn.

Just before dark she heard a flapping of wings outside the grating of her prison. She ran to the bars and saw her youngest brother there. She wanted to cry out to him for help, but she said nothing. He lifted his wings and flew away again.

Next morning a great fire had been prepared and she was led out to it on a cart. She had her coats of mail over her arm, and as the cart was being pulled along, she sewed. Right up to the time that she was drawn to the fire, she sewed as if nothing else mattered. Only one sleeve remained.

The crowd jeered. "Take her evil magic away from her!" they shouted.

But as they ran forward to seize the coats of mail there came a wild beating of wings around their heads, making the air turn cold as snow. The eleven swans circled round and the townspeople ducked and cowered and ran for shelter. Quickly Snow-rose threw the coats of mail over her brothers.

The spell was broken. Eleven young men stood beside her, and the youngest had a swan's wing instead of an arm.

Snow-rose stood up and faced her prince. "I am innocent," she said.

The bells of the town rang for seven days. The eleven brothers danced at the wedding of the prince and his bride, but the wicked queen wasn't there. Oh no. She had been thrown on the fire.